MY PARENTS ARE GETTING DIVORCED AND IT'S NOT MY FAULT

by

Robert Kahn

Illustrated by Daniel Majan

Gotham Books
30 N Gould St.
Ste. 20820, Sheridan, WY 82801
https://gothambooksinc.com/

Phone: 1 (307) 464-7800

Published by Gotham Books (August 05, 2022)

ISBN: 979-8-88775-025-5 (sc)
ISBN: 979-8-88775-026-2 (e)

Hello Mandee, why are you sitting here and crying?

Oh Bobby, it is terrible and I know that it is all my fault. If I just hadn't been born, or if I could move to another home, this wouldn't be happening.

Come on Mandee, stop crying and tell me what is wrong.

Well Bobby you know how Mom and Dad have been really unhappy and fighting a lot lately?

Yes, it has made life really rough at our house, and I wish they would get along.

Last night I heard them fighting again and they are going to get a DIVORCE!

I just know this is all my fault.

You're right Mandee, this is the worst thing that has ever happened to us. I wish it wasn't happening. But, it isn't your fault.

13

It isn't, are you sure Bobby?

Yes I am Mandee, let me explain. When Mom and Dad first met, they started dating.

They fell in love and they wanted all their friends to know how happy they were. They decided to get married.

They had a wedding and all of their friends were there. Then they went on their honeymoon.

The years went by and they had two children, you and me.

We are getting older and growing-up. Unfortunately the love between Mom and Dad didn't grow or get stronger.

Pretty soon they were unhappy and this caused more problems. Soon the fighting started and has continued. Now the love between them has changed and they feel that a divorce is the answer.

TRUST

There are many reasons that parents get divorced. It is never just one reason they come to this decision, but many reasons.

The hard part is still ahead of us. The 4 of us won't be living together anymore. Mom and Dad will each have their own place. Sometimes we will live with Mom and sometimes we will live with Dad.

Divorce is very hard emotionally on everyone. The parents getting divorced, their children, and everyone who cares about that family. But sometimes it is the answer and everyone benefits.

There won't be any more fighting since they will be living apart. This will make our lives at home better.

But sometimes we will be very sad. When this happens, you should talk to a trusted adult. This trusted adult will listen and help you feel better to cope with this situation.

GUIDANCE COUNSELOR

One trusted adult that you can always talk to is the school counselor. They are trained to help children feel better when they have a situation like this one.

And always remember, even though Mom and Dad won't be married, they both still love us very much.

QUESTIONS:

1. Why was Mandee sad at the beginning of the book?
answer on page 8

2. What did Mandee think was the reason for the divorce?
answer on page 10

3. Is it really Mandee's fault?
answer on page 12

4. What did Bobby tell Mandee why their parents were really getting divorced?
answer on page 24

5. What is one of the hardest part to deal with divorced parents?
answer on page 30

6. Who are people that will be effected by a divorce?
answer on page 32

7. Who is a trusted adult that you can tell a problem to.
answer on page 38

8. If your parents are getting divorced, are they divorcing you?
answer on page 40